D1608230

REDLINE

THE REACHER EXPERIMENT BOOK 6

Jude Hardin

1

Way back in the middle part of the twenty-first century, around the time Rock Wahlman was born, practically every filling station in the country had been fitted with charging ports for electric vehicles. The batteries that provided the power to propel those cars and trucks from one place to another had gotten more and more sophisticated over the decades—even more so in recent years—and now, in the summer of 2098, in the United States of America and in many other nations around the world, you could drive up and plug in and be fully charged in about five minutes.

But you needed a credit card.

And Rock Wahlman didn't have a credit card.

He paid cash for everything, and in the summer of 2098 you could still find places that would accept cash for gasoline purchases, and that was why he had traded his SUV for another vehicle with an internal combustion engine, a compact sedan this time. He couldn't sleep in the sedan, as he had in the SUV on occasion, and he sometimes banged his right knee on the steering wheel climbing in and out, but the little car was pretty fast and it was cheap to drive and you could back it into one of the narrowest spots in a parking garage if you needed to disappear for a few days.

Those were the thoughts going through Wahlman's mind as he cruised past the exit for Greensboro, North Carolina, at four o'clock in the afternoon on the eighth of July. Those were his thoughts, but he didn't actually say any of those things to the man sitting in the passenger seat.

"I just like the sound of a real motor," Wahlman said, trying to explain why he'd purchased a car that ran on gasoline, trying to keep the conversation to a minimum.

"Electric motors are real," the man said. "And they're better for the environment."

The man sitting in the passenger seat seemed to know a lot about the environment. He seemed to know a lot about everything. He was getting along in years. Probably in his eighties, Wahlman guessed. The skin on his face was an odd shade of yellow, what you might come up with if you mixed some mustard into a cup of tea, and his eyes looked as though someone might have dribbled broken egg yolks into them. He had been walking backward along the edge of the highway, facing traffic, holding a cardboard sign that said *MYRTLE BEACH.* Wahlman wasn't planning on going anywhere near that area, but he figured he could get the guy a hundred miles or so closer to the coast, and he figured every little bit helped.

Wahlman was on his way to visit an old friend, a fellow Master-At-Arms who'd settled down in Virginia after retiring from the Navy. The guy had been pretty good with

2

computers, and he knew other guys who were pretty good with computers, and Wahlman was hoping that he might be able to assist him in gaining access to some classified information. Maybe the old friend could help. Maybe he couldn't. It was worth a try.

Wahlman had stopped and picked up the hitchhiker about an hour ago. Now he was starting to wish he hadn't. The guy talked too much, and he smelled like cigarettes and rotgut whiskey.

"I'll be getting off the interstate and heading north in a few minutes," Wahlman said. "Want me to drop you off at the next exit?"

"I wouldn't mind going all the way to Norfolk with you, if that's okay."

"Norfolk is north of here. Since you're trying to get to Myrtle Beach—"

"I can catch a bus for next to nothing in Norfolk," the man said. "It's a straight shot, right down the coast."

"Okay," Wahlman said.

He reached over to turn on the radio, hoping it would keep the old man from talking so much.

It didn't.

"I've been sitting here beside you for over an hour, and I don't even know your name," the man said.

"Wendell."

It was the name on Wahlman's latest fake driver's license. Wendell P. Callahan. Wahlman didn't know what the *P* stood for. He figured he would just make something up if anyone ever asked.

3

"I'm Rusty," the man said. "That's what my friends always called me, anyway. Back when I had friends who were still alive. Back when I had hair that was still red."

Rusty chuckled, his laughter quickly turning to a cough, the kind of gurgling hack that sounds like there might be something seriously wrong, the kind that you try to hold your breath for when you're passing by the person doing the hacking in a grocery store aisle.

"You okay?" Wahlman said.

"I'm okay. You got a tissue or something?"

"Glovebox."

Rusty opened the glove compartment, reached in and pulled out a couple of paper napkins that Wahlman had saved from couple of different fast food joints. Rusty coughed into the napkins, and then he wadded them up and tossed them on the floorboard.

"Bet you can't guess why I'm going to Myrtle Beach," he said.

"Why would I want to guess?" Wahlman said. "It's none of my business."

"Just thought you might be curious."

Rusty coughed again. A narrow thread of bright red blood tricked down from the corner of his lips. He wiped it off with his shirt sleeve.

Wahlman had seen a lot of things as a law enforcement officer in the Navy. He had a strong stomach. There wasn't much that bothered him. A guy sitting inches away and coughing up blood was one of the things that did. He switched off the radio. He thought about pulling over and handing Rusty a twenty and making him get out of the car right there. But he didn't. He felt sorry for the old guy. It was obvious that he didn't have a lot of time left.

"All right," Wahlman said. "Tell me why you're going to Myrtle Beach."

"Maybe I shouldn't tell you, come to think of it."

"Okay."

"It's kind of a secret, if you want to know the truth."

"Okay."

"I guess I could tell you. But you have to promise not to tell anyone else. I signed some papers, and I could get into big trouble if anyone ever—"

"Tell me or don't tell me," Wahlman said. "It doesn't matter to me."

"You promise not to say anything to anyone about it?"

"I promise."

Rusty reached into one of his pockets and pulled out a piece of peppermint candy, the kind you see in bowls on cashiers' counters at diners sometimes. He peeled off the cellophane and slid the sugary red and white disk into his mouth. He didn't offer Wahlman a piece. Maybe it was his last one. He contemplatively twisted the sticky little wrapper with his thumbs and forefingers for a few seconds, and then he flicked it on the floor next to the soggy napkins.

"Let me just start by saying that I'm a veteran," he said. "Army. They're the ones responsible for the shape I'm in right now, and they're the ones who'll be footing the bill to fix me up."

Wahlman wondered what kind of medical procedure

could possibly benefit a man of Rusty's advanced age, a man with such glaringly obvious health issues. Doctors could do some pretty spectacular things with some pretty spectacular equipment these days, but their knowledge and skills and technological expertise could still only go so far. They still hadn't developed a remedy for the human condition commonly known as TMB—*Too Many Birthdays.* They still hadn't found a cure for that. Not that Wahlman had ever heard about.

But then maybe he hadn't heard about everything.

He sat there with his eyes on the road and his hands on the wheel and listened while Rusty talked.

2

Rusty said that he'd recently celebrated his ninetieth birthday. Which meant that he'd been born in 2008. Which meant that he was almost fifty years older than Wahlman. He'd experienced things that Wahlman had only read about in history books. He'd seen driverless cars and thought-enhancing brain implants and flying robots that could do everything from changing a flat tire to delivering a baby. He'd seen all of that come and go. He'd seen technological advances that surely must have seemed like a good idea at the time but that had ultimately done more harm than good.

"Teleportation," Wahlman said. "That was the last straw, right? That was when the leaders of the world got together and decided that everything needed to be dialed back a notch."

"Ten notches was more like it," Rusty said. "But yeah. When they figured out how to disassemble and reassemble inanimate objects at a molecular level, and when they figured out how to use specially-designed satellites and lasers to move those objects from one part of the planet to another, that was a big game changer. It revolutionized the shipping industry, for one thing. You could go online and order a couch or whatever and have it delivered to your living room in a matter of seconds."

"Sounds great."

"Sure. It was great. But it was all done with computers. Ninety-nine percent of it, anyway. Unemployment skyrocketed. Most of the positions that had been crucial to that particular industry were suddenly obsolete. Then other industries were affected. Just about everything you can think of. It all started toppling, like a row of dominoes. It all came too fast. The human race just wasn't ready for it."

"The schematics for those types of satellites and lasers are probably locked in an underground vault somewhere," Wahlman said. "It's only a matter of time until—"

"I don't think so," Rusty said. "And I'll tell you why. If you can move a couch through space and plop it down in the middle of a living room, then you can move a bomb through space and plop it down in the middle of a city. That was where we were heading. They hadn't figured out how to do it with nukes, but they probably would have eventually."

"Not possible, from what I've read."

"A lot of things are not possible, until suddenly they are. Anyway, the technology of the day only worked with inorganic material, so biological weapons were out, but certain enemy factions had started experimenting with a variety of chemicals. That's why I'm coughing right now. I was exposed to KAP-Blue on the battlefield one time."

"KAP-Blue?"

"Look it up. You'll find it on some of the conspiracy theory sites. Nasty shit. It'll take your ass out in a heartbeat. The Army hasn't officially admitted that it exists, but I can tell you that it does."

"If you were exposed to it, then how—"

"I was wearing full protective gear, but the respirators they were issuing to non-coms at the time turned out to be defective. I know for a fact that I didn't breathe in much of that shit. If I had, I would have been dead. But I inhaled enough of it to make me sick."

"That must have been decades ago," Wahlman said. "How do you know that being exposed to KAP-Blue was responsible for your current condition?"

"They found traces of the compound in my liver," Rusty said. "It was right there in black and white on the lab report. There was no way the Army could deny it. That's why I'm on my way to Myrtle Beach right now. The Army's performing some clinical trials down there. Experimental shit. I volunteered for it. I probably won't live through the procedure, but maybe what they learn from me will be beneficial to some other soldiers in the future. That's the way it works with science sometimes, right? Trial and error."

Experimental shit. That got Wahlman's attention. Now he was genuinely interested in what Rusty had to say.

Last year, in October, Wahlman discovered that he was an exact genetic duplicate of a former Army officer named Jack Reacher. The cells used to produce Wahlman had been taken from Reacher in 1983, over a hundred years ago. Reacher had been in Beirut, Lebanon at the time. In a hospital. Wounded. A phlebotomist had drawn some blood from him and some other officers one morning and had sent the specimens to a lab back in the States. Cells were extracted and cryogenically preserved, and then they were used for cloning experiments decades later.

Now someone was trying to hide the fact that any of that had ever taken place.

A secret experiment carried out by the Army was the reason Wahlman existed, and it was the reason that a current Army officer going by the name of Dorland was trying to make sure that he stopped existing. There had been another clone. A man named Darrell Renfro. He was dead now. Murdered. Wahlman knew that he would be next. There had been several attempts on his life already. He'd been forced to abandon his home, and his best friend had been killed, and the woman he loved had brought their relationship to a screeching halt, concerned for the welfare of her family. He needed to get to the bottom of why all this was happening, and he needed to try to put a stop to it.

"What kind of experimental shit?" he said.

"They're going to give me a new heart, and a new liver, and a new pair of lungs."

"What's so unusual about that?"

"Plenty," Rusty said.

But he refused to elaborate any further.

Because of the papers he'd signed.

"How do I know you're not just making all this up?" Wahlman said.

"Why would I do that?" Rusty said.

"I don't know. That's what I've been trying to figure out. Maybe you think I'll be curious enough to drive you all the way down to Myrtle Beach. Then maybe you'll climb out of my car and have a good laugh on the way to the nearest liquor store."

"Well?"

"Well what?"

"Are you curious enough to drive me all the way down to Myrtle Beach?"

"Maybe," Wahlman said. "I'm still thinking about it."

But Wahlman wasn't really still thinking about it.

He'd made up his mind already.

He was going to Myrtle Beach.

3

Since April, when the elite military intelligence unit he was in charge of bugged out of their secret complex in the Mojave Desert and relocated to Tennessee, Colonel Dorland had been living alone in a one-room cabin on the edge of a cliff. He liked it up there, for the most part. It was extremely private, and on a clear day you could walk out onto the deck and see for miles.

July 8 was a clear day.

But Colonel Dorland wasn't seeing what he wanted to see.

"Too much foliage this time of year," Lieutenant Talfin said, stepping up to the railing and gesturing out toward the landscape. "But I can assure you that it's down there. You can probably see the roof, right here from your deck, in the late fall and winter, after the trees lose their leaves. No telling what you might be able to see with a telescope that time of year, or even a good pair of binoculars."

Talfin had broken the news to Colonel Dorland over the phone a couple of hours ago. There was a fairly large lake at the bottom of the mountain, down in the valley, and according to Talfin, a very nice house had been built on a thirty-acre parcel of land that skirted the shore. Kasey Stielson's parents owned the property, and Kasey and her daughter had been staying there with them until recently. Apparently Rock Wahlman had been staying there too, at least for a while. His fingerprints were all over the place.

Colonel Dorland could see part of the lake from his deck, but he couldn't see the house.

"Why are we just now finding out about this?" he said.

"The deed was registered under a corporate name. Kasey's father owns several—"

"Where's Kasey's father now?"

"We don't know, sir. The whole family's gone. They must have found another—"

"We're supposed to be an intelligence unit," Colonel Dorland said. "We're supposed to be the best in the world at this kind of shit. You're telling me that Wahlman was right under my nose. He was right down there in that valley, less than five miles away, and I didn't even know it. This phase of our operation could have been completed months ago. Yet here we stand with our clueless collective thumbs up our clueless collective asses. Do you know what kind of shit storm I'm likely to be facing because of this, Lieutenant Talfin? Do you have any idea?"

"We'll find them, sir. It's just going to take a little more time."

This wasn't the first time that Talfin had dropped the ball, or even the second time. He was the kind of officer who was really smart when it came to books. Second in his class at WestPoint, first in his class at MCO—the Army's two-year program for newly-commissioned officers interested in careers that involved covert operations. He was extremely knowledgeable, but he didn't seem to be able to put much of that knowledge to use when it came to practical applications. He'd been in charge of cyber security at the facility in California. After the breach that prompted the Code Charlie Foxtrot and the subsequent emergency location change, Dorland had allowed him to continue working with the unit as Second Research Officer. So far, he'd managed to maintain the rank of lieutenant, but he'd been skating on thin ice for quite some time now.

And the ice just kept getting thinner.

"Just remember that shit rolls downhill," Colonel Dorland said. "Get off my porch. I want a written report on my desk by zero seven hundred tomorrow morning. Think you can handle that?"

"Yes, sir."

Talfin saluted, and then he walked back through the cabin and exited through the front door.

Dorland pulled his cell phone out of his pocket and pressed the *SEND* button on a text message he'd composed earlier. He heard Lieutenant Talfin start his car, and he heard the sound of rubber on gravel as he backed out of the driveway. And that was all he heard. He didn't hear Talfin skidding to a stop when he got to the roadblock a mile or so down the mountain, and he didn't hear Talfin shout and scream as he was being dragged out of his vehicle and forced to walk into the woods. He didn't hear any of that, and he certainly didn't hear the gunshot that drove a bullet into Talfin's brain, because the staff sergeant he'd sent the message to always used a sound suppressor on these types of occasions.

4

The alleged facility where the alleged experiments were taking place wasn't actually located within the Myrtle Beach city limits. It was on a small island, a couple of miles off the coast. Only accessible by boat or helicopter.

Wahlman steered away from the ticket booth and joined a line of cars and trucks waiting to board the ferry. The flow of traffic was being regulated by a signal at the edge of the boarding ramp. It changed from red to green when the crew was ready for another car to make its way up onto the parking deck. The boat had probably been around for a century or so, but it appeared to be in pretty good shape. In fact, there were parts of it that appeared to be brand new. The original diesel inboards had been replaced with solar-tidal hybrids from a company called Motion-Prop, and the decks had been coated with a gritty heat-absorbing compound that had only been around for a few years. Wahlman was impressed. Too many vessels from that era were sold for scrap or intentionally sunk and left to rust away at the bottom of the ocean. It was nice to see one that had been properly refurbished.

Wahlman lifted his foot from the brake, allowing his car to inch forward as one of the vehicles ahead of him boarded the ferry. He looked over at Rusty, who was screwing the cap back onto a half-pint bottle that was a little less than half full.

"I'm curious as to why the Army didn't provide transportation for you," Wahlman said.

"They sent me some money," Rusty said. "I used it for other things. Necessities."

"Food and shelter are necessities. Whiskey and cigarettes are not."

Rusty shrugged. "Are you going to lecture me now?" he said.

"No," Wahlman said. "But weren't you concerned that you wouldn't be able to get here in time?"

"I'm not scheduled to report until tomorrow morning. So I'm actually going to be early."

"That's not what I meant," Wahlman said.

Rusty seemed puzzled for a few seconds. Then it sunk in.

"Oh," he said. "You meant that I could have died while I was out there on the road, trying to hitch a ride. To tell you the truth, the thought never really crossed my mind."

Wahlman inched forward some more. He was next up to board the ferry. The light turned green and he eased the sedan up the ramp and onto the parking deck. One of the crew members directed him toward the last available slot, a cramped sliver of space between a black pickup truck and a gray SUV.

"What do you think?" Wahlman said.

"Looks pretty tight," Rusty said. "We might have to wait for the next ferry."

Wahlman didn't feel like waiting. He had to back up and pull forward a couple of times, but he finally managed to squeeze into the spot. He switched off the engine, glanced into the rearview mirror and saw another one of the crew members dragging a heavy steel chain across the boarding lane. The crew member secured the chain, and then he distributed three orange traffic cones along the length of it. A few minutes later, the ferry pulled away from the ramp and started moving out into the bay.

"I'm going to get out and walk around for a while," Wahlman said.

"Mind if I join you?"

"It's a free country."

"That's right. And some of us fought to keep it that way."

Wahlman thought about telling Rusty that he too was a veteran, that he too had engaged in multiple fierce battles in multiple faraway places, that he'd taken the oath and had served honorably and had experienced more horrific action in twenty years than anyone should experience in twenty lifetimes. He thought about telling Rusty those things, but he didn't. He reminded himself that he was on the run, living under an alias. The more you say about yourself in a situation like that, the more likely you are to be caught in a lie. So you say as little as possible. You talk to as few people as possible. And when you do talk to someone, you say things that can't easily be verified.

Wahlman climbed out of the car. There was a walkway

along the starboard side of the ferry, a platform about as wide as a diving board, and there were two signs bolted to the railing, a rectangular one that said *TO OBSERVATION DECK,* and an arrow-shaped one that said *ONE WAY PEDESTRIAN TRAFFIC.* There was an identical platform on the port side, but there was only one sign on the railing over there. It said *DO NOT ENTER.* Which made it obvious to Wahlman that the platform on the port side was for getting back to the parking deck. Sort of like walking around the block, everyone moving counterclockwise, keeping people from having to squeeze past each other on the narrow pathways.

The observation deck was a flat rectangular area about half the size of a tennis court. It overlooked the lane on the bow where all of the vehicles would eventually disembark. There was a ladder on the starboard side to get up there, and one on the port side to get down. One-way traffic. Just like the platforms. Wahlman stepped up to the railing and gazed out over the choppy water. The sun was behind him, low in the sky, and there was a warm breeze blowing up from the south.

"It's nice out here," Wahlman said, turning and noticing that Rusty had stopped a few feet short of the railing. He was standing there with his arms folded, staring down at the textured deck.

"I don't like the water," he said. "Never have."

"The railing is solid steel," Wahlman said. "It's bolted to the deck. There's nothing to worry about."

"I'd rather keep my distance."

"You can swim, right?"

"No. And I have no desire to learn how. You can put me on an airplane and hand me a parachute and tell me to jump out over enemy territory, and I'll have no problem with that. Just don't tell me to jump into the deep end of a pool. Or even the shallow end. Not going to happen."

Wahlman was just the opposite. He was okay with water. Not that he was any sort of great swimmer, but he could tread water for hours if he needed to, and he could get from one end of a pool to another easily enough with his own clumsy version of the backstroke. But he didn't care for heights. Especially the kind Rusty was talking about. Jumping out of a perfectly good airplane didn't make a lot of sense to him. You find a proper landing strip, and then you find a car and go wherever it is you need to go. That was how that worked.

"What else are you afraid of?" Wahlman said.

"Doctors. That's why I've been trying to stay drunk for the past few days. I gave up alcohol and tobacco years ago. But this shit is making me nervous. You know what I mean?"

"Yeah. I guess it would make me nervous too."

A tone sounded through the loudspeakers, and a pleasant-but-obviously-mechanical male voice announced that the ferry would be docking in approximately ten minutes.

"Please return to your vehicles now," the robot said, its programmed sing-song inflections dripping with faux enthusiasm. "And don't forget your safety belts!"

Wahlman turned and started walking toward the portside ladder.

Rusty didn't move.

"Let's go," Wahlman said.

"I'm not feeling very well," Rusty said.

"Because of the water?"

"I guess so."

Wahlman looked around. The other passengers who'd been enjoying the observation deck were gone now. He and Rusty were the only ones left.

"You can't just stand out there in the middle of the deck while the boat mates up with the ramp," Wahlman said. "It's not safe."

"Nothing is safe," Rusty said.

"Take a deep breath. You'll be fine."

Rusty nodded. He took a deep breath, and then he followed Wahlman around to the ladder and down to the pathway. He shuffled along slowly, gripping the railing with one hand and Wahlman's shirttails with the other.

The breeze had picked up, and Wahlman had to hold onto the baseball cap he was wearing to prevent it from ending up in the water. As they made their way back to the parking area, Rusty started coughing again, and when Wahlman stepped up to his car to open the doors, Rusty started walking around in circles and mumbling incomprehensibly out on the open end of the deck.

"Arno snow la bertiga," he said. "Arno snow la bertiga!"

"Get in the car," Wahlman said.

But Rusty didn't get into the car. A pained expression washed over his face, and a fat stream of bright red blood shot out of his mouth, and he spit and coughed and staggered toward the stern and twirled past the orange traffic cones and stumbled into the heavy steel chain and did a little backflip and splashed headfirst into the churning froth.

5

Colonel Dorland hadn't felt particularly good about sending out the order to eliminate Lieutenant Talfin, but he hadn't felt particularly bad about it either. The truth was, he hadn't had much of a choice in the matter. Talfin had proven himself to be a bungling bonehead on multiple occasions, and you can't just reassign a guy like that to a supply outfit or something. Once you make it to a certain level in the intelligence community—once you know practically every government secret there is to know—you can't expect to just walk away and pretend to be a regular old officer doing a regular old job. Talfin had been perfectly aware of what he was signing up for from the beginning. And with the recent severe errors he'd committed, he had probably known what was coming. When you make the choice to inhabit the extremely specialized covert world of military intelligence and then follow that choice with gross incompetence, you might as well stick your head between your legs and kiss your ass goodbye. That was the way it worked. Every time. No exceptions.

At any rate, Colonel Dorland didn't have time to dwell on it. He was packing some uniforms and some civilian clothes into a suitcase and a garment bag, getting ready to go on a little trip. Not a vacation, exactly, although he planned on getting in a few rounds of golf while he was away. He was stuffing some socks and underwear into the top left corner of the suitcase when his cell phone trilled.

It was Foss.

Colonel Dorland picked up.

"Hello, General," he said.

"Just wanted to follow up on our previous conversation," General Foss said. "I assume you're on your way."

"There was a pressing matter I needed to take care of earlier this afternoon, so I'm getting sort of a late start. I'm packing some things right now. I'll be on the road in less than an hour."

"What kind of pressing matter? Is it something I need to know about?"

"No, sir. It was just a personnel issue. It's all taken care of now."

General Foss sneezed, not bothering to cover his phone's mouthpiece with his hand as he did so. The abrupt cacophonous blast did a number on Colonel Dorland's left ear.

"It's getting kind of late," General Foss said. "Our first patient is scheduled to report first thing in the morning. I was hoping you could be there with the others to greet him."

"I'll be there," Dorland said. "Looking forward to it."

"Good. It's quite the momentous occasion. It's what

we've been working toward for a long time, and now it's finally going to happen. And of course this is only the beginning."

"It's an amazing time. That's for sure."

Colonel Dorland was trying to sound as excited about the project as General Foss undoubtedly expected him to sound. Dorland truly was excited about it, and it truly was an amazing time, and it truly was only the beginning.

But there was still one problem.

One loose thread.

General Foss didn't know that Rock Wahlman was still out there. He was under the impression that the matter had been taken care of months ago.

General Foss had given Colonel Dorland a strict deadline, and Colonel Dorland had managed to confirm the kill with DNA specimens, but the specimens had not actually been taken from Wahlman. They'd been taken from the other clone. From Darrell Renfro. Since both of the men had been produced with cells that had originated from the same unsuspecting donor, both of the men had ended up sharing the exact same DNA. Which had made the deception relatively easy. The technician working the graveyard shift at the city morgue in New Orleans didn't make a lot of money, so it wasn't very difficult to persuade him to give up a couple of vials of blood and a couple of tissue samples. Not very difficult at all.

At the time, with the deadline looming, Dorland had been certain that Wahlman would be eliminated in a matter of days. He'd paid a lot of money to make sure of it. When it didn't happen, he couldn't just admit to General Foss that he'd tampered with the DNA samples. If he ever admitted to that—to purposefully falsifying a Priority-1 intelligence report that had been funneled directly to a superior officer— he might as well stick his own head between his own legs and kiss his own ass goodbye.

So the deception continued, but it couldn't continue indefinitely. The risks kept getting greater, and the stakes kept getting higher, and Dorland was more determined than ever to find Wahlman and take him out of the picture. Wahlman's existence threatened to disrupt the flow of cash being pumped into the current project, and it threatened to disrupt the flow of blood being pumped into Colonel Dorland's arteries. Wahlman had to go, and it had to be soon.

"Are you still there?" General Foss said.

"Yes, sir. Sorry. I was just thinking about how exciting this project is. I can't wait to get down there and see everything for myself."

"You're going to love it," General Foss said. "What we're going to accomplish at that facility is going to go down as one of the most marvelous achievements in human history. It's an honor to be a part of something like this. It's a great time to be alive."

"It certainly is," Colonel Dorland said. "It certainly is."

6

Wahlman ran to the chain. He got down on his hands and knees and leaned over the edge of the deck and stared down into the bubbling wake. After several seconds of foamy gray nothingness, he got up and grabbed one of the life preservers from the railing and was about to jump in when a pale blood-streaked hand floated by and stopped him in his tracks. The hand was attached to a wrist and the wrist was attached to a forearm and the forearm was attached to nothing. The swirling tide gripped the severed limb and rocked it back and forth, making it appear as though it was waving goodbye.

Which, in a sense, it was.

The rest of Rusty's lifeless form surfaced and tumbled around in the forceful stream of the engines before following the arm into the murky depths of the bay. It was a gruesome sight. The old man's head had been twisted around so that his face and his ass were pointing in the same direction. It was the kind of image that you can never fully forget, the kind that's likely to show up in nightmares from time to time, the kind that makes your heart feel like it's going to beat its way right out of your chest.

Wahlman thought about calling for help.

There were two reasons he decided not to.

Rusty was gone, and there was nothing anyone could do to bring him back. That was one reason. The other was somewhat selfish. If Wahlman called for help, the captain of the boat would have to report the incident to the police. The detectives assigned to the case would want to talk to Wahlman, and eventually they would want to scan his driver's license. The guy Wahlman had bought the license from had guaranteed that it was clean, but Wahlman didn't want to bet his life on it. If Wendell P. Callahan had one unpaid parking ticket, the detectives would then have probable cause to dig deeper, and there was no telling what kinds of problems might follow from there.

Extradition to Louisiana on a first-degree murder charge came to mind.

So Wahlman didn't call for help. He slid the life preserver back onto its hook and walked to his car and climbed in and stared at the rear bumper on the cargo van parked in front of him. He was relieved that all of the vehicles on the ferry were facing the bow, making it unlikely that anyone had witnessed what had happened to Rusty. The corpse would eventually float to the surface, but Wahlman doubted that there would be much of an investigation. Not for a ninety-year-old man with a whiskey bottle in his pocket. There would be an obligatory report written up and a halfhearted effort to locate any next-of-kin, and there would be a three-inch column in the metro section of the local newspaper, and that would be that.

Only that wouldn't be that.

Not in this case.

Not if Rusty had been telling the truth.

Because if Rusty had been telling the truth, some people were expecting him to show up first thing in the morning. Military people. On the island. At some sort of secret research facility. Out in the middle of nowhere. Doctors, nurses, technicians, everyone eager to get started on whatever it was they were going to do.

A new heart, and a new liver, and a new pair of lungs.

But not an ordinary series of transplants.

Something special.

Something experimental.

The procedure had been explained and the forms had been signed and the money for transportation had been sent. It was a done deal. Rusty was supposed to be there, and the United States Army was going to be mighty interested in knowing why he wasn't.

Which meant that Wahlman didn't have much time.

He needed to find the facility, and he needed to find out exactly what was going on there, and he needed to do it before the staff started showing up for the day.

7

It was dark by the time Wahlman made it off the boat. He wanted to get an idea of the layout of the island. He didn't have a cell phone or any other device that might have helped with navigation, so he stopped at a filling station and walked inside and asked if they had any maps.

They didn't.

"You can check at the place across the street," the clerk said. "They used to have maps."

Wahlman checked at the place across the street. They didn't have any maps either. The young man standing behind the counter didn't even seem to know what Wahlman was talking about.

"A roadmap," Wahlman said. "It's a big piece of paper with squiggly lines all over it. You open it and look at it for a while, and then you try to fold it back the way it was, but you never can so—"

"Why can't you fold it back the way it was?" the young man said.

"Because you can't. It's just one of those things. Like

perpetual motion. It's scientifically impossible."

The young man shrugged.

Wahlman filled his tank and bought a hotdog and a bag of chips and drove around for a while and got lost for a while and ended up back at the ferry dock, where he'd started.

He drove up to the ticket booth.

The attendant slid the window open. He was enormously fat and his head was shaved completely bald. He was eating a sandwich. A giant sub. Lots of meat and fresh vegetables and the bread looked fresh. Wahlman was still hungry. He'd taken one bite of the hotdog and had thrown the rest away.

The attendant wiped his mouth with a paper napkin.

"Can I help you?" he said.

"When's the next ferry?" Wahlman said.

"Ten minutes or so. You want a ticket?"

"If I buy a ticket now, can I use it later?"

"It's good for twenty-four hours."

"Okay. I'll take one."

Wahlman handed the attendant some cash. The attendant printed a ticket and handed it to Wahlman.

"Have a nice night," the attendant said.

"Do you know of a place around here that sells roadmaps?" Wahlman said.

"Not right offhand. Where you trying to go?"

Wahlman hesitated for a few seconds. He couldn't exactly tell the guy the truth. He couldn't tell him that he was looking for a secret research facility being run by the United States Army. He couldn't tell him that he was planning to nose around and try to find out what the Army was up to. He couldn't tell him that all he knew about the place was that it was somewhere on the island, somewhere out in the middle of nowhere.

Wahlman couldn't tell the attendant any of that. But he figured that the facility would be guarded, and he figured that the guards would be military guys, and he figured that some of those guys would be young and single, and he knew from experience that a certain percentage of those young and single guys tended to gravitate toward certain types of establishments when they were off duty.

"Nowhere in particular," Wahlman said. "I'm just looking to have a good time tonight. If you know what I mean."

"I'm not sure that I do," the attendant said.

"You know. Have a few drinks. Maybe talk to some women."

"Third Avenue," the attendant said.

"How do I get there?"

The attendant gave Wahlman directions.

"Just watch yourself," the attendant said. "Some of those places over there are kind of rough."

"Okay. Thanks."

"No problem. Have a nice night."

"I have one more question," Wahlman said.

"Yeah?"

"Where did you get that sandwich?"

8

It was like Bourbon Street on steroids.

Drums thumping, guitars wailing, vocalists screaming emphatically about everything from eating their favorite breakfast cereal to having their nipples twisted off with pliers. The music coming from one of the clubs was so loud it seemed to make the sidewalks vibrate. There were massage parlors and tattoo parlors and pool halls and smoke shops. There were hotels where you could rent a room for the night, and there were others where you could rent a room for an hour. Neon everywhere, street vendors on every corner.

Wahlman bought a can of beer and sat on a bench outside a t-shirt shop. He had known that none of the Army guys would be in uniform, but it didn't matter. He'd been a Master-At-Arms in the Navy for twenty years, and he could spot active duty military personnel a mile away. He could see it in the way they walked. The way they carried themselves. And if he got close enough, he could see it in their eyes. He could usually tell the lifers from the short-timers, and he could usually tell A.J. Squared Away from Joe Shit The Rag Man.

The guy who walked out of the t-shirt shop probably fell somewhere in the middle. Wahlman figured that he did what he was supposed to do, but that he rarely went above and beyond. He wore fashionably-tattered jeans and a sleeveless gray hoodie with black lightning bolts printed on the sides. He had an earring in each ear and a tattoo on each arm and he could have used a haircut. He wasn't a perfect soldier, but he wasn't a dirt bag either. Just an average guy.

As he was stepping toward the curb, Wahlman stood and turned, intentionally bumping into him, intentionally spilling some beer on his nice gray shirt.

"Sorry," Wahlman said.

"I just bought this shirt, asshole."

The guy stared down at the stain. He was carrying a crumpled paper bag with the shop's logo printed on it. Wahlman figured that he'd bought the gray hoodie there and had stuffed the shirt he'd been wearing into the bag.

"Sorry," Wahlman said again.

"You're going to be really sorry when I shove that beer can up your—"

Wahlman reached out and grabbed the guy's wrist and dug his thumb into a pressure point. The guy dropped the bag and his knees buckled and he curled into a fetal position there on the sidewalk. All in about two seconds.

"You're not going to shove anything anywhere," Wahlman said. "Who's your commanding officer?"

"What?"

"Did I stutter? Who's your CO? Where do you work?"

"You an MP or something?"

34

"Who's your CO?"

"Look, man, let's just forget about it, okay? You go your way and I'll go mine and—"

"Answer my questions or I'm going to break the wrist. Then, after I drive you to the emergency room, I'm going to drive you to Beaufort and lock your sorry ass up."

"What do you want from me?"

"Where do you work?"

The guy's ears were turning purple. He looked like he might be getting ready to puke. The people passing by didn't seem to be paying any attention. Business as usual. Just another Army guy squirming on the sidewalk, being busted for whatever.

Wahlman dug his thumb in deeper.

"All right," the guy said. "I'm working here on the island. Guard duty."

"Where?"

"It's a concrete building, over off Highway Thirty. It doesn't really have a name. Not that I know of. Everyone just calls it The Box."

"Who's your CO?"

"Major Combs. She's in charge of the guard detail."

"Combs. Like the kind you comb your hair with?"

"Right."

"What are you guarding? What's going on inside the concrete building?"

"I'm on TDY. They don't tell me things like that."

TDY. Temporary duty. It didn't sound right. Not for an installation where secret experiments were taking place.

Special clearances would be required. Not worth it for someone who was only going to be there for a short time. It sounded like something the guy had been coached to say.

Wahlman could have tried to coax the truth out of him, but he didn't want to take the time. He needed to get away from there before a city cop or an MP showed up.

He eased off the pressure point.

"What's your name?" he said.

"Bridges."

"Like the kind you drive a car over?"

"Yeah. Or the kind you jump off of, if you're me right now."

Bridges looked genuinely concerned about what might happen next. And of course he would have had good reason to be apprehensive if Wahlman had still been an active duty Master-At-Arms. If Wahlman had still been on active duty, Bridges would have been in handcuffs by now.

"I'm going to let you off with a warning this time," Wahlman said.

"A warning?"

"Just try to maintain some military bearing from now on, whether you're in uniform or not. You never know who you might be dealing with."

"Yes, sir."

"I'm not a sir. You can call me Senior Chief."

"Yes, Senior Chief."

Bridges stood and brushed himself off. He cupped his wrist in his hand, trying to massage some of the pain away. Wahlman leaned over and picked up the crumpled paper bag and handed it to him.

"Beat it," Wahlman said.

Bridges nodded. He stepped off the curb and headed toward the nightclub where the extremely loud music was playing.

9

Colonel Dorland had only been driving for a couple of hours, but he was already starting to get sleepy. He was accustomed to going to bed early and getting up early. It had been a long time since he'd pulled an all-nighter, and that was exactly what this was going to be. Nine and a half hours from his cabin in Tennessee to the research facility off the coast of South Carolina. Nine and a half hours, if everything went perfectly. Which it rarely did, on a trip that long. There was usually at least one major traffic snag along the way. Which meant that nine and a half hours was an optimistic estimate. Ten hours was more likely, maybe even eleven.

General Foss had denied Colonel Dorland's request for a helicopter. The general had reminded him that The Box was a Top Secret facility, and that any movement to and from The Box should be considered Top Secret as well. Dorland hadn't pressed the issue, but it seemed to him that a helicopter ride to Myrtle Beach and a rental car from there would have been secret enough. Now he was going to have to stay awake all night, and he was going to have to be all smiles and handshakes and exaggerated enthusiasm for the dog and pony show that was supposed to start at seven o'clock in the morning.

Not that the research being conducted at the facility wasn't a big deal. It was. But not quite as big as Foss made it out to be. Not in Dorland's opinion. There's really only one first time for everything, no matter how much you pretend otherwise. You can never really erase the truth. You can bury it and hope that it's never revealed, but you can never eliminate it completely. Not as long as one person still knows every little detail behind what really happened, along with every little detail behind the conspiracy to conceal what really happened. Not as long as one person still has every little detail recorded on a flash drive.

Dorland stopped at a filling station and hooked his car up to one of the chargers. He walked inside and used the restroom, and then he purchased a large coffee and two chocolate donuts and a six pack of energy drinks and some chewing gum and walked back out to his car. As he was sliding the coffee cup into the cup holder on the center console and tossing the brown paper bag that contained the other items onto the passenger seat, his phone started vibrating in his pocket. He was expecting it to be Foss again. Checking up on him again. It wasn't Foss. The caller ID said *UNKNOWN*.

Which was strange.

In fact, it was unprecedented.

Colonel Dorland's cell phone, the one he used for official communications with select members of the intelligence community, had been engineered in a secret underground laboratory in Colorado. It operated on secure frequencies. There were only a handful of people on the planet who knew the number, which was updated weekly, along with the voice and text encryption codes. The odds of that particular device receiving a call from anyone other than General Foss or one of the senior members of Colonel Dorland's staff were a trillion to one.

Yet there it was.

UNKNOWN.

Dorland decided that it must be some kind of glitch. The caller ID must have malfunctioned. There was no other explanation.

It was probably Foss again. Checking up on Dorland again.

Dorland decided to answer the call.

It wasn't Foss.

It was a woman.

She only said one word.

"Run," she said.

And then she hung up.

10

Wahlman had parked his car on Main Street, two and a half blocks east of Third Avenue. As he turned the corner and started heading away from the hubbub, he heard footsteps coming up from behind him. Three guys. He knew that there were three of them without having to turn around. He could tell by the sound of their shoes on the pavement. Three military guys. He knew that they were military because they had fallen in step with each other. Force of habit. From marching drills.

Wahlman didn't speed up, but he didn't slow down either. He kept a steady pace. The guys got closer. Maybe they were expecting Wahlman move to the side, step off onto the street so they could pass by.

Wahlman didn't move to the side.

He stayed in the middle of the sidewalk. It was just as much his as it was theirs. If they wanted to pass by as a group, they were the ones who were going to have to step off onto the street.

"Hey," one of the guys said.

Wahlman didn't turn around.

"Hey you," another one of the guys said.

Wahlman still didn't turn around.

"Hey Senior Chief," the third guy said.

Wahlman recognized the voice. It was Bridges, the guy he'd muscled the information out of a few minutes ago.

Wahlman stopped walking. He stood there with his back to the guys. Which was a gamble. They could have clubbed him in the head. Or knifed him in the back. They could have jumped on him and taken him to the pavement and beat him to a pulp. But they didn't. They knew that he could handle himself. Bridges had told them all about it. They were under the impression that they were dealing with a Senior Chief Petty Officer, a Master-At-Arms in the United States Navy. They were under the impression that they could get in a lot of trouble if things didn't go their way.

"What do you want?" Wahlman said, still not bothering to turn around.

"I was just wondering if I could see your military ID," Bridges said.

"What for?"

"We have strict orders not to tell anyone where we work," one of the other guys said. "We just need to know that you really are who you say you are."

"I didn't say I was anybody."

"You said you were a Senior Chief," Bridges said.

"I said you can call me that," Wahlman said. "It's not my fault you jumped to conclusions."

"So you're not a Senior Chief?"

"You guys should march on back to the club. While you're still able."

"Impersonating an officer," Bridges said. "That's a pretty serious—"

Before Bridges could finish his sentence, before the neurological network connecting his brain to his lips and vocal chords could fire off the nearly-instantaneous impulses it was going to take for him to form and articulate the word *offense*, Wahlman turned around and came down hard on the bridge of his nose with a closed fist. There was a sickening wet crunch, like the sound of a raw egg being smashed with a mallet.

Bridges staggered backward. Bright red blood gushed from both of his nostrils and his eyes rolled back in his head and he crumpled to the sidewalk in a heap.

Bridges had been standing between the other two guys.

Bonehead One and Bonehead Two.

Wahlman could tell that Bonehead One had consumed quite a bit of alcohol. His eyes were bloodshot and fearless. He was probably around six feet tall, and he probably weighed around two hundred pounds. He had a slim waist and broad shoulders and biceps the size of grapefruits. Bonehead Two was much smaller. Five-eight, one sixty. He didn't look to be much of a threat, but Wahlman knew that looks could be deceiving. One of the lessons he'd learned as a Master-At-Arms was to never underestimate an opponent, not even one who is eight inches shorter and seventy pounds lighter than you are. Guys like that can surprise you sometimes, compensating for their disadvantage in size with speed and technique. If you're not careful, guys like that can kill you with their bare hands in a split second.

Both of the off-duty soldiers stood there with looks of astonishment on their faces. Then Bonehead One pulled something out of his pocket. It could have been a small pistol or a canister of pepper spray or a set of brass knuckles, but it wasn't any of those things. It was a knife. A switchblade. Cheap and disposable and deadly. Similar to the weapon Wahlman had been on the wrong end of in Barstow, California a few months ago. So similar that it gave him a momentary sense of *deja-vu.*

Bonehead One thumbed the little button on the side of the mother-of-pearl handle, allowing the shiny silver blade to spring free and lock into place. He didn't say anything, but there was something in his eyes that made his intentions obvious. He wasn't planning to hurt Wahlman. He was planning to kill him. He gripped the handle and started slicing the air in front of him, moving forward with slow and heavy steps, his motions sloppy and stupid, like some kind of angry and disoriented wild predator, like a hibernating bear that had been jabbed with a stick.

In Barstow, Wahlman had defended himself with a park bench. This time, there was nothing like that within reach.

But there was something better.

Bonehead Two.

As Bonehead One advanced with the knife, Wahlman took a quick step to the left and planted the heel of a size fourteen leather work boot into Bonehead Two's solar plexus. Stunned and suddenly unable to breathe very well,

Bonehead Two stumbled backward and tripped over his own feet and landed on his ass at the edge of the curb. Wahlman reached down and grabbed his ankles and swung him like a baseball bat, slamming the top of his skull into Bonehead One's jaw. The results of the impact were impressive, even to Wahlman, who had seen practically every kind of horror that human beings are capable of inflicting on each other. The knife skittered into the gutter and Bonehead One spun around and wobbled over to a grassy area and started spitting out teeth. He stood there for a while, and then he sat down and crossed his legs and stared blankly into the distance.

Bonehead Two appeared to be unconscious. His eyelids kept fluttering and his fingers kept making little jerky movements and he was probably unaware that he was being held upside down and that blood from the gash in his forehead was dripping onto the sidewalk like a leaky faucet. Wahlman carried him over to the grassy area and lowered the back of his head onto Bonehead One's lap, and then he dropped the rest of him onto the ground.

Bridges was starting to wake up. He rolled onto his side and coughed and wiped some of the blood off of his face with the sleeveless gray hoodie.

Wahlman walked over to where he was lying.

"Still want to see my military ID?" Wahlman said.

"I'm going to let you off with a warning this time," Bridges said.

Then he passed out again.

Wahlman picked up the knife and folded the blade into

the handle. He slid the weapon into his pocket and walked to his car and climbed in and started the engine. He eased away from the curb and headed west, back toward the dock, back toward the turnoff he'd seen for Highway 30.

11

Colonel Dorland sat there and stared down at his phone for a few seconds, wondering exactly how such a call could have gotten through. Wondering exactly what the caller had been expecting to accomplish.

Run.

What was Dorland supposed to run from? His duty as the commanding officer of an elite intelligence unit in the United States Army? That wasn't going to happen. Only cowards shirked their sworn duties, and Colonel Dorland was no coward. He realized that he had problems, and that he was going to have bigger problems if General Foss ever found out about the Wahlman situation, but he was determined to see this thing through, determined to make everything right, determined to come out smelling like a rose in the end.

The successful completion of this assignment would undoubtedly result in a promotion, and the next step up was a big one.

Brigadier General.

Dorland liked the sound of it. He could see himself wearing the uniform. He wanted that star more than he'd ever wanted anything. It was what he'd spent his entire career working toward. It was where he wanted to be.

And it was where he was going to be.

He wanted the promotion more than anything, which basically meant that he wanted Wahlman dead more than anything. Wahlman was the only roadblock at this point. Once that situation was taken care of, all kinds of good things were bound to happen.

Dorland had decided that he was going to have to take care of the matter himself. He was going to have to get his hands dirty. He had a plan, and he was going to put that plan into action as soon as he was finished with his obligations down at The Box. Day after tomorrow, if everything went well.

Right now he needed to talk to the officer in charge of the night watch, back at the headquarters in Tennessee. Lieutenant Driessman, if he remembered correctly. Driessman was new. Colonel Dorland hadn't had a chance to go through his file yet, so he didn't know a lot about him, but like everyone else assigned to the unit, he'd been checked out thoroughly by the personnel division. Which meant that he was a top-notch officer and one hundred percent loyal to the United States of America. Dorland tapped in the number for the duty phone, got an answer on the first ring.

"Hello, Colonel Dorland. How are you tonight, sir?"

"Driessman?"

"Yes, sir."

"Someone called my cell phone a few minutes ago," Dorland said. "I need to find out who it was."

"Someone called your secure line?"

"Right."

"Someone who's not on your list of contacts?"

"Right."

"I can check into that for you, sir. It might take a few hours. Of course I'll need the access codes for your phone."

Dorland gave him the codes, knowing that everything stored on the processor for more than a week was protected by several extra layers of encryption.

"Call me as soon as you know something," Dorland said.

"Yes, sir."

Dorland clicked off.

He stared at his phone some more, and then he peeled the lid off of his coffee cup and took a sip. The coffee was bitter, and it wasn't very hot, but Dorland didn't really need it anymore anyway. He wasn't sleepy anymore. He was wide awake now. He grabbed a napkin and one of the chocolate doughnuts from the bag on the passenger seat, and then he started his car and headed back out to the interstate.

12

Highway 30 was still under construction. One of the signs planted along the shoulder said that it was eventually going to be an Official United States of America Toll Road. Right now it was free. Which was good. Official United States of America Toll Roads required electronic passes, and electronic passes required proper identification, and the Department of Transportation guys who did the checking were experts at spotting fakes. Rock Wahlman avoided driving on Official United States Toll Roads like he avoided eating spoiled fish. For a man in his situation, purchasing one of those passes would have been tantamount to turning himself in, and turning himself in would have been tantamount to signing his own execution warrant. Not going to happen. So he was happy to know that the road was still free for now, happy to continue moving forward.

The highway sliced through the heart of a pine forest for about twenty miles inland, and then it turned to dirt. Several A-frame barricades with blinking yellow lights on top of them separated the paved part from the dirt part. Beyond the barricades, off to the side, there were some dump trucks and bulldozers and concrete mixers that had been parked for the night, along with a singlewide trailer that probably served as an office for the foremen and engineers. Wahlman figured that the crew would be back at it bright and early.

He turned his car around and headed back the other way. He'd driven the entire twenty miles, and he hadn't seen anything that even remotely resembled what Bridges had described. Which meant that Bridges had been lying, or that there was a turnoff somewhere that Wahlman had missed. He drove back to where the highway started, and then he drove all the way to the barricades again. Nothing. No turnoff. He turned around again and headed back the other way again. He thought about finding Bridges and breaking his nose again.

Then he saw it.

There was a slight opening in the tree line, a semicircle that had been carved into the thick tangle of vines and underbrush. Like a tunnel, with dense foliage serving as the walls and ceiling. The opening was only wide enough for one vehicle, and it was nearly invisible from the highway. If Wahlman hadn't been driving close to thirty miles an hour under the posted speed limit, and if he hadn't been intensely focused on finding anything out of the ordinary, he never would have seen it. Like one of those pictures where you're supposed to find a hidden object. If nobody tells you there's a basketball somewhere in the wagonload of pumpkins, you're probably not going to notice it.

Wahlman drove about half a mile past the opening, and

then he veered off into the grass and parked at the edge of the woods. He broke some branches and ripped out some vines and draped everything over the side of the little sedan in an effort to camouflage it. There hadn't been any streetlights installed on the highway yet, so he figured he was good to go until daybreak, which was still several hours away.

He crept along the tree line until he made it back to the opening, and then he got down on his belly and turned the corner and crawled through. A few feet past the mouth of the tunnel there was an enormous steel sign bolted to two steel posts.

AUTHORIZED PERSONNEL ONLY.

Huge red letters. Reflective paint. The sign said some other things directly beneath the red letters, in smaller print that was black. Something about this being an official United States government facility. Something about trespassers being shot on sight.

Wahlman ignored the warnings and continued using his knees and elbows to propel himself deeper into the tunnel. It doglegged to the left, and then it led to a clearing with a guard shack and a heavy-duty chain-link gate connected to a heavy-duty chain-link fence.

Barbed wire. Razor ribbon.

A lone sentry stood outside the shack. He was wearing combat gear. Vest, helmet, the works. There was a pistol strapped to his right hip, and an assault rifle slung over his right shoulder. Night vision scope, thirty-round magazine. The guy was holding a tablet computer, swiping and tapping, probably documenting that all was secure. He probably did it every thirty minutes. Maybe more often than that at a place like this. Maybe every fifteen. He seemed focused and alert and ready to do whatever it took to defend his post.

The building that Bridges had described was about thirty yards beyond the gate. It was immediately obvious to Wahlman why they called it The Box. It was a concrete cube about as wide as an average convenience store and about twice as tall. No windows, no doors. Not that Wahlman could see. There had to be a way in and out, of course. Maybe on the other side. Or maybe the Army had brought back the technology for teleportation, and maybe they had figured out how to use it on living beings this time. Maybe they had figured out how to do it without turning a person into a quivering pile of gelatinous goo. Wahlman was lying there on his belly pondering the possibility when he saw the silhouette of a man walking along the edge of the roof.

Another guard. Another vest and helmet and pistol and rifle.

On top of the building.

So maybe that was it. Maybe there was some kind of hatch up there. It made sense. A single portal on the roof would make the facility virtually impenetrable to outsiders. One way in, one way out. Great for security. Not so great if you needed to evacuate everyone in a hurry.

Wahlman took a few seconds to consider what such a blatant disregard for safety might or might not mean, and then he shifted his gaze to the left and stared into the forest.

He wanted to do some scouting before he decided on how to proceed. He wanted to walk into the woods and recon the perimeter of the property. He wanted to see the sides of the building, and he wanted to see what was in back. He wanted to see if there were more guards. More than the one standing outside the shack and the one on the roof. He wanted to know if there was a ladder bolted somewhere along the concrete façade. And if there was a ladder, he wanted to know exactly where it was, in case he needed to get to it in a hurry.

He wanted to do some scouting, but he couldn't. The underbrush was too thick. It would have taken him hours to make it all the way around the building. Even with a machete, which he didn't have. All he had was Bonehead One's cheap little switchblade. Not much help against vines as thick as ropes.

Another guard appeared outside the shack. Now there were two of them. They were talking, but Wahlman couldn't hear what they were saying. The guy who'd been there first gave the other guy the rifle and the pistol and the tablet computer.

Apparently they were changing shifts.

The guy who'd been there first walked into the shack. Wahlman figured he was going in there to get his things, his lunchbox and his keys and whatnot, and that he would be back out momentarily. But he wasn't. Not after five minutes. Not after ten. Wahlman wondered what the guy was doing, and then it occurred to him that maybe the guy wasn't even in there anymore. Maybe he was on his way home. Back to the barracks, or wherever he stayed when he wasn't on duty.

Wahlman hadn't seen the second guy walk up to the shack. His appearance had been sort of sudden. He'd shown up at some point while Wahlman was staring into the woods. Wahlman had only taken his eyes off the shack for a brief period. Thirty seconds, maybe less.

Interesting.

Maybe there was an underground tunnel, a passageway that connected the guard shack to the main building. Maybe the tunnel went all the way to the back of the building, and maybe there was a parking area back there and an alternate route out to the highway.

Maybe there was indeed a hatch on the roof, but maybe that wasn't the only one. Maybe there were two guard shacks, one on each end of the property, and maybe there was a portal inside each of the shacks, and maybe there were tunnels connecting everything to everything.

Wahlman mapped it all out in his head. He was only guessing, of course, but it seemed like a feasible layout. It seemed like overkill, but maybe whatever was inside the big concrete building warranted such extravagant security measures. Maybe whatever was inside the big concrete building was the biggest and best-kept secret in the history of the world.

Wahlman tried to shake off the hyperbolic thoughts. The truth was, a certain amount of money had been allocated to build the facility. When you're in charge of something like that and you're given a certain budget to work with, you tend to make sure that there's nothing left by the time you're finished. You tend to spend every penny. You don't want to give any of it back. It's the way it works in the military, and in the private sector—all the way down to average guys with average jobs asking their wives for permission to take a little out of savings to build a game room in the basement. You spend what you have, because you're not likely to get more anytime soon.

So it was possible that the absurdly tight security measures were a product of over budgeting. Then again, it was possible that the government was hiding something truly remarkable and unprecedented. Something that might be of great interest to Rock Wahlman. Something that might shed some light on his current predicament.

He needed to know.

He was trying to figure out a way to get inside the guard shack without having to kill the guard when a bright orange flash of light reflected sharply off a strip of razor ribbon and a searing bolt of pain drilled its way into the right side of his neck.

Wahlman immediately knew what had happened. He knew that he'd been shot. The guy on the roof must have spotted him with the night vision scope.

The guy had fired one shot.

The guy had nailed it.

Wahlman could feel the blood trickling down his throat. He figured the bullet had clipped his right jugular vein. He figured it wasn't the kind of wound that he was likely to recover from. He figured it was the kind that was likely to kill him.

Then he knew. He knew that this was it. The world got narrow, and then it was just a little white dot, and then it disappeared completely.

13

Colonel Dorland never heard back from Lieutenant Driessman. He decided to let it go for now. He had too many other things to think about. He made it to the research facility at 06:04. There was a sentry posted at the front transport module, just outside the fence line. The young soldier popped to attention and saluted and pressed the button to open the gate. Dorland returned the salute and drove through and steered around to the back of the building and parked his car. There were plenty of spaces. The doctors and nurses and technicians hadn't shown up for work yet. Dorland figured the parking lot would start filling up in another thirty minutes or so. He switched off the engine and climbed out of the car and walked up to the rear transport module, as General Foss had instructed him to do.

The exterior facades of the front and rear modules were identical. They were designed to look like ordinary guard shacks. Wood-frame construction, metal roofing panels, lapboard siding. A PFC wearing a dress blue uniform stepped out onto the concrete apron and saluted.

"Good morning, sir," he said.

"Good morning. Are you my escort?"

"Yes, sir."

"Do you have a name, soldier?"

"Yes, sir. Sorry, sir. My name is Watley, sir."

Watley was about six feet tall, and he appeared to be in excellent physical condition. He wore eyeglasses with thick black plastic frames, the kind they issue in basic training. Which indicated to Dorland that he probably hadn't been in the military very long. Hardly anyone kept those frames for longer than a paycheck or two. There was an Expert Marksman badge pinned above his left breast pocket. Impressive for someone just out of boot camp.

"I was told that a guy named Bridges was going to be my escort," Colonel Dorland said. "What happened to him?"

"Private Bridges didn't show up for duty this morning, sir."

"Why not?"

"We're not sure yet, sir."

"Is someone looking for him?"

"Yes, sir. A detail was sent out about an hour ago."

Dorland nodded. "All right," he said. "Where to first?"

"I need to get you checked in at the security office. They'll give you a temporary ID badge and a list of codes for the electronic locks."

"Then what?"

"I'll give you a complete tour of the facility. Our first patient is due to report no later than zero seven hundred, and—"

"We'll welcome him aboard with a special breakfast in the chow hall at eight," Dorland said. "I already know about that."

"Yes, sir."

Watley pushed his eyeglasses up on the bridge of his nose, and then he just stood there and stared out at nothing. He'd been alert and attentive up to that point, but now he seemed to be off in another world.

"Well?" Dorland said.

"Sir?"

"Let's get on with it, Private. We don't have all day."

"Yes, sir."

Dorland followed Watley into the transport module. The interior of the space was unfinished. Bare studs, plywood flooring. It looked like a good place to store your rakes and shovels and hedge trimmers. But Dorland knew better. He'd been briefed on these types of modules. He'd read the manuals and watched the videos. He knew what to expect. He knew what was coming next.

There was a fingerprint scanner and a keypad mounted to one of the studs. Watley punched some numbers into the keypad, and then he pressed his right forefinger against the scanner. A section of the floor opened up and a transparent capsule appeared, a sealed chamber about as wide as a porch swing and about as tall as a kitchen countertop. There were two bucket seats inside the oblong bubble, each equipped with a hinged shoulder harness and a head and neck stabilizer cushion. Kind of like the seats you see on some of the more elaborate rollercoasters at some of the more elaborate amusement parks. The seat to Dorland's right was marked *OPERATOR,* and the seat to his left was marked *PASSENGER.* Above the headrests there was a sign that said *WEIGHT LIMIT 500 POUNDS.*

"This is my first time in one of these things," Dorland said. "I understand it can get kind of rough."

"It's not too bad, once you get used to it," Watley said. "Have you eaten anything this morning?"

"I had a couple of energy drinks in the car."

"Do you ever experience motion sickness?"

"Not usually."

"Are you claustrophobic?"

Dorland hesitated for a second.

"No," he said.

"Great. You should be fine."

Watley opened the capsule and motioned for Colonel Dorland to climb in.

"Has anyone ever died doing this?" Dorland said.

"No. It's actually much safer than the old setups they used in installations like this. Catwalks and ladders and whatnot. The capsule is unbreakable. You could drop it from an airplane and it wouldn't crack."

"What if it did crack?"

"You mean while we're riding in it?"

"Yes."

"Our heads would explode," Watley said. "That's what I've heard, anyway. From the sudden change in pressure. I don't know if it's true or not."

Colonel Dorland took a deep breath, and then he climbed down into the passenger seat.

14

Wahlman woke up strapped to a gurney. A blue towel had been draped over his groin area. Otherwise, he was naked. There was a big round reflective light shining down on him, the kind they use in operating rooms. To his right there was a wall of shelves, the syringes and cotton balls and tongue depressors and other medical supplies visible through a series of heavy glass doors. To his left there was rolling bedside table with a plastic pitcher and a plastic drinking cup on it. Next to the table there was a guard with a machinegun.

Wahlman tested the leather cuffs and tethers securing his wrists and ankles, decided right away that there was no way for him to break free.

"Where am I?" he said.

The guard didn't say anything. He just stood there gazing expressionlessly into the glass cabinets, the barrel of his rifle pointed directly at Wahlman's core.

Wahlman was having trouble remembering what had happened to him. Then it all came flooding back.

He'd been shot.

In the neck.

A double set of doors swung inward and a woman walked into the room. A military woman. Army. Late thirties or early forties. Dress blues, hair pinned back tightly. She was slender and prim and the expression on her face was one of fierce determination, like a thoroughbred running a close second heading into the stretch. There was a semi-automatic pistol holstered above her right hip. The soles and heels of her patent leather shoes clicked pertly on the hard rubber floor tiles as she stepped up to the gurney.

"I'm Major Combs," she said. "I have some questions for you."

"I have some questions for you, too," Wahlman said.

Major Combs laced her fingers together and rested them at the front of her midsection.

"Okay," she said. "You go first."

"It's cold in here," Wahlman said. "Could I have a blanket or something?"

"Maybe. In a little while. If you cooperate."

"Where am I?"

"The infirmary."

"Could you be a little more specific?"

"No."

Wahlman glanced over at the guard. He hadn't moved. He was still staring across the room. Toward the shelves. Toward a stack of plastic wash basins.

"Why am I still alive?" Wahlman said.

"What do you mean?"

"The sign in the woods said—"

"It says that trespassers will be shot on sight," Major Combs said. "It doesn't say that they will be killed on sight."

"So what are we talking about? Rubber bullets?"

"Micro-darts. Loaded with a certain type of medication."

"Like a tranquilizer? Like the kind of shit they—"

"More sophisticated than an ordinary tranquilizer. But yes, the effects are similar."

"I tasted blood," Wahlman said.

"You tasted the medication as it entered your bloodstream. Like an IV bolus from a syringe."

"So I didn't need surgery?"

"No. You needed a square of gauze and a strip of tape. Which you got. Now it's my turn to ask some questions, and your turn to provide some answers. Why were you trying to infiltrate our facility?"

"I don't know what you're talking about," Wahlman said.

"Don't lie to me. Who are you working for?"

"I'm not working for anyone."

"Why were you trying to infiltrate our facility?"

"You already asked me that."

Major Combs was only a foot or so away from the table. Wahlman could smell the soap she'd used to wash herself with that morning. There was a very plain wristwatch on her left wrist. Black leather band, stainless steel housing. There were no rings on her fingers.

"Our infrared surveillance cameras recorded everything you did," she said. "You covered your car with vines and branches, and then you walked along the edge of the woods until you came to our entryway, and then you—"

"The most you can charge me with is trespassing," Wahlman said. "And I really don't see that going anywhere. In fact, I think I could make a pretty good case that my rights were violated."

"You ignored our sign."

"I was traveling alone on a dark and unfamiliar highway. I had car trouble. I hid my vehicle because it's all I have and I was worried that someone might try to steal it. I started walking toward town, but it was a long way back. Ten miles or more. I was tired and thirsty and I didn't think I was going to make it. I desperately needed some help, and when I ran across a place where I thought there might be some people, I naturally gravitated toward that place. I could barely stand up, so I got down on my belly and crawled. I was too weak to look up and read a sign. I didn't even see it. I crawled right past it. I got a little scared when I saw the guys with guns, so I decided to stop and wait and think it over for a while. Next thing I know, someone has taken all my clothes and strapped me to a—"

"You need to answer my questions," Major Combs said. "I'm trying to be reasonable, but my patience is wearing thin. If I can't get any answers from you, I'll send someone in who can."

"I'm not in the military," Wahlman said. "You don't have any authority over me. If you want to bring one of the local police agencies in, you can tell them your version of what happened, and I'll tell them mine. I'll be sure to tell them that I was injected with some kind of drug that knocked me out for a few hours."

Major Combs didn't say anything. She turned and exited the room. She didn't order the armed guard to follow her, but he did anyway. As if it was expected. Prearranged. As if something very discreet was about to happen. Something the guard wasn't supposed to see.

Wahlman tested the leather restraints again. There was a little bit of play in the ones binding his wrists. He could lift his arms a few inches off the table, but he couldn't pull his hands through the cuffs, no matter how hard he tried. They were buckled too tightly.

Wahlman tried to relax. Tried to think. The bright overhead light and the aftereffects of the drug he'd been injected with made it difficult to concentrate. Not to mention the monotonous electrical hum coming from one of the glass cabinets. The one in the corner. The one furthest from the door. Wahlman wondered if that section of the unit was refrigerated. He figured it was. Dozens of plastic containers were stacked up in there. The containers were not marked. Wahlman had no idea what was inside them. Some sort of medication, he guessed. His mind kept wandering. He couldn't seem to stay focused on one thing for more than a few seconds at a time. He thought about Highway 30. About how dark it was. About how he'd traveled back and forth and hadn't seen any businesses or any other vehicles. He thought about Kasey, about how much he still missed her.

A guy wearing white scrubs and a white lab coat walked in. Early twenties, average height. Broad shoulders and a thick middle and a double chin. He had dark hair and an immature mustache, everything trimmed to military specs, but just barely. He could have used a trip to the barber shop and about a hundred trips to the gym. He covered Wahlman's legs and torso with a wool blanket, and then he wheeled the bedside table closer to the gurney.

"I'm going to be your nurse today," the guy said. "I need to insert an INT, and I need to change your dressing, and I need to draw some blood."

"What's an INT?" Wahlman said.

"An IV site. Peripheral. You know, in one of your arms."

"I don't want that," Wahlman said. "You need to let me go."

"Sorry. Doctor's orders."

The guy started pulling some things out of his pockets. He had a packet of gauze and a roll of surgical tape and a pair of bandage scissors. He had a rubber tourniquet and some individual alcohol wipes that were sealed in little foil packets. He had a pair of surgical gloves and some glass vials for the blood specimens and a plastic and cardboard blister pack with a sterile eighteen-gauge IV needle in it and a syringe that had been filled with some sort of clear liquid. He grabbed the gloves and stretched one over each hand and started lining everything up in neat little rows on the bedside table. It took him a couple of minutes to get everything just right. Just the way he wanted it.

"You're making a big mistake," Wahlman said.

"Don't worry," the guy said. "Everything's going to be fine."

He picked up the roll of surgical tape and tore off a piece that was about four inches long. He ripped the piece in half, lengthwise, creating two narrower strips that were identical in length. He stuck the ends of the two narrow strips to the edge of the table, allowing them to dangle there like a couple of translucent streamers. He tied the tourniquet around the upper part of Wahlman's right arm, and then he tore open one of the foil packets and pulled out the alcohol wipe that was inside it and leaned in to find a vein.

He leaned in a little too far.

In one swift and violent motion, Wahlman arched his back and neck and head-butted the guy just above his left ear. It was a brutal bone-to-bone blow. It sounded like a bat hitting a ball. The impact gave Wahlman an immediate headache. It gave the guy in white scrubs an immediate skull fracture. The guy slumped over Wahlman's abdomen, and then he slid to the floor like a sack of potatoes.

Wahlman reached for the bedside table, but the tether that connected the cuff on his right wrist to the frame of the gurney wasn't quite long enough. He could brush the edge of the table with the tip of his middle finger, but that was as close as he could get. He strained and pulled and jerked and stretched, but it was no use. He wanted the bandage scissors. He wanted them as much as he'd ever wanted anything. They were as crucial to him as the air he was breathing. They were his ticket to freedom. They were his only chance.

He wasn't cold anymore. Sweat was dripping down his face. His head was throbbing and he was starting to feel some numbness in his right arm. Pins and needles. Because of the tourniquet. He thought he might be able to stretch down and untie it with his teeth, but his range of motion was limited by the restraints, and by the bulk of the muscles in his chest and shoulders. He took a deep breath. He was trying not to panic. Trying to think of a way out of this. He wasn't ready to give up. He would never do that. But he wasn't delusional either. The odds were against him. A million to one, maybe. If he could get to the scissors. Which he couldn't. He stretched again. Strained again. Brushed the tip of his finger against the edge of the bedside table again.

Then something wonderful happened.

The guy on the floor grunted, and then he must have rolled over or shifted his position in some other manner. Wahlman couldn't see the guy, but he could hear him. There was a rattle in his throat every time he took a breath. Maybe he was dying. Maybe his damaged brain had sent out some emergency signals to the muscles in his arms and legs in a last ditch effort to survive. To run away. Like the jerky spasms you have sometimes when you're dreaming. Whatever the case, the movement he'd made had caused the table to roll a little closer to the gurney. Now Wahlman could reach it. Easily. He gripped the edge with his thumb and forefinger and pulled it in closer.

There were three rows of supplies. The items the guy had planned to use to start the INT were in the front row, and the items he'd planned to use for the blood draw were in the middle.

The scissors were in back.

Way in back.

They must have slid when the table moved. They weren't in line with the packet of gauze anymore. They were closer to the edge.

Wahlman grabbed the blister pack and used it to extend his reach. He thought it was going to work. He thought he had this now. But he didn't. He couldn't pull the scissors closer to his fingers. The blades were pointed toward him, and he couldn't get any traction against the slick stainless steel. He set the blister pack down and grabbed one of the strips of tape dangling from the front of the table. His fingers were numb. He could barely feel what he was doing. He managed to crumple the strip of tape into a sticky little ball, and then he managed to press the sticky little ball onto the edge of the blister pack.

He reached for the scissors again, using the contraption he'd assembled. It worked. The sticky little ball stuck to the shiny steel blades, allowing him to guide the cutting tool toward the gurney. A sense of elation washed over him. He felt like celebrating. He felt like whooping and hollering. He fumbled around for a few seconds and finally managed to get his fingers through the handles of the scissors and he curled his right wrist as far as it would curl and he snipped the tether and proceeded to snip the others until all four of his limbs were free. He untied the tourniquet and sat up, fighting off a wave of vertigo as he pivoted and planted his bare feet on the cold rubber tiles.

Then he heard footsteps in the distance, clicking pertly.

15

The chow hall was packed, but nobody was saying much.

Colonel Dorland stared down at his breakfast plate. Scrambled eggs, bacon, biscuits, hash browns. There were several doctors and scientists sitting at the table with him, including the geneticist who'd developed the formula for the growth medium and the surgeon who'd perfected the actual procedure. There were colorful plastic balloons taped to the walls and colorful paper streamers tacked to the ceiling. Over in the far right corner of the room, there was a guy sitting at a grand piano, but he wasn't playing anything.

Because the party hadn't officially started yet.

Because the guest of honor hadn't arrived yet.

Dorland took a sip of coffee from the ceramic mug next to his plate. He looked at his watch, and then he turned and locked eyes with PFC Watley, who was sitting at the next table over.

"It's eight-thirty already," Dorland said. "How long are we supposed to wait?"

"I'll call the security office again," Watley said. "Maybe

he's down there checking in right now."

"Why wasn't someone assigned to escort him from his home to the facility? That's what I don't understand. Seems like a no-brainer, for something this important."

"Sir, I don't—"

"What was the name of the officer I met with earlier? The one in charge of security?"

"That was Major Combs, sir."

"Get her on the phone. Tell her I want to talk to her. ASAP."

"Yes, sir."

Watley pulled out a cell phone and punched in some numbers. He had a brief conversation with someone on the other end, and then he clicked off.

"Well?" Colonel Dorland said.

"She's not in the office right now," Watley said. "She's on her way to the infirmary."

"What's wrong with her?"

"She's okay. There's a—"

"How do I get to the infirmary?"

"I can go with you if you want me to, sir. Or I can try to reach Major Combs on her cell phone."

Colonel Dorland considered those options, decided against them. Major Combs needed to be counselled, but there was no point in making a public display of it. There was no point in embarrassing her in front of her subordinates.

"The things I need to say to her need to be said in person," Dorland said. "And in private. I can manage on my own. Just tell me how to get there."

16

Wahlman needed a weapon.

Fast.

He tied the blanket around his waist and stepped over to the glassed-in storage area, to the unit in the corner that seemed to be refrigerated. He was hoping that the plastic bins stacked up in there were full of micro-darts and that the micro-darts had been loaded with the same medication that had been used to knock him out. He pulled on the door, but it didn't open. It was locked. There was a keypad and a card scanner mounted to the side of the unit. Wahlman figured you had to scan your ID and punch in a code to get the door to open. Alternatively, you could walk back over to the gurney and grab the blue towel and wrap it around your fist and break the glass. Probably not the recommended method, but effective nonetheless.

Wahlman reached in and grabbed one of the containers. It wasn't filled with medication. It was filled with plastic IV bags, and the plastic IV bags were filled with blood. For transfusions. Fat paper labels had been glued onto the bags, indicating the blood type and the Rh factor. Below the stack of plastic bins there was a drawer marked *PATIENT BELONGINGS*. Wahlman opened the drawer and reached in and ferreted through the pile, found his wallet and his keys. He figured the drawer was located in that particular cabinet in case patients brought medications from home that needed to be refrigerated. He set his things on the bedside table and grabbed the scissors. Someone had taken the time and energy to donate the unit of blood he was holding. Someone had endured the pain of the needle. Someone had risked the potential side effects. It was a generous thing to do. A caring thing. It was a dirty rotten shame to waste even one drop, but Wahlman didn't feel as though he had any choice. He cut one of the corners off the bag and walked over to the double set of doors and squirted the entire unit on the floor. He retreated back to the bedside table and quickly fashioned a shank using some gauze and some tape and a shard of glass from the broken cabinet. A few seconds later the doors swung open and Major Combs and a short skinny guy carrying a red toolbox walked in and promptly proceeded to slip and fall on their asses. Wahlman darted over there and crouched down and held the shank to Major Combs's throat and unsnapped her holster and pulled out the pistol.

"Be careful with that," Major Combs said. "It's loaded with real bullets."

"You're going to do exactly what I tell you to do," Wahlman said. "Or two of those real bullets are going to come out real fast."

Wahlman held the gun on Major Combs and the guy who'd walked in with her and tossed them the scissors and the blue towel and the roll of surgical tape and gave them specific instructions on how to gag each other and tie each other up. Once most of the work was done, Wahlman finished it off by taping Major Combs's wrists together behind her back.

The nurse was still on the floor, over by the gurney. His breathing sounded a little better than it had earlier. Still pretty ragged, but better. Wahlman pulled the guy's shoes off and his scrub pants and his lab coat and slid into everything as quickly as he could. There was a phone and an ID card in the left front pants pocket. The guy's name was Sebley. He was a second lieutenant. The shoes were a little tight and the sleeves on the lab coat were a little short, but Wahlman wasn't complaining. It could have been worse. They could have sent a female nurse, and the female nurse could have been wearing a dress. Then Wahlman would have been forced to try to escape naked. So he wasn't complaining, and he wasn't nearly as curious about what was going on at the facility as he had been last night. Getting out of there in one piece was the only thing on his mind at the moment. Then maybe he could investigate from a distance. Maybe get some interest from the media. There was definitely a story here. Wahlman still had no idea what it was, but he knew it was something big. Something that the Army was devoting a great amount of time and effort and money to conceal.

The lab coat had some fairly large patch pockets sewn

onto the front, just below the waistline, one on each side of the snaps. Sebley had been carrying his supplies in them. They were empty now. Wahlman dropped his wallet and his keys into the pocket on the left side. He kept a grip on the pistol and slid his right hand into the pocket on the right side and stepped over the slippery puddle of blood he'd created and exited the room.

The hallway appeared to be about fifty feet long. It was covered with some sort of industrial-grade vinyl. Green. Pale and dull. The kind of stuff that would probably last a thousand years. There were wooden doors on both sides of it, marked with numbers. Wahlman could see the end of it. He could see that it doglegged to the right. He strolled along at a steady pace. Not too fast, not too slow. He didn't want to draw attention to himself. He was just a nurse, a staff member, heading from one area to another. No big deal. Eyes forward, one foot in front of the other. He was hoping that there was an exit right around the corner. Or an elevator. Or a stairway. He was hoping that he wouldn't run into anyone on the way out.

But he did run into someone.

Literally.

As soon as he turned the corner.

17

The guy Wahlman bumped into was less than six feet tall. Five-eight, five-nine maybe. He was a colonel. Full-bird. Blue eyes, bald on top, gray around the temples. Dress blues, lots of ribbons. There was a lanyard around his neck. Attached to the lanyard there was a transparent plastic sleeve, and inside the sleeve there was an identification card.

VIP
TEMPORARY
DORLAND, J.L.
UNITED STATES ARMY

Wahlman's heart did a flip flop. He stared down at the card and read it again, just to make sure.

It was him.

It was Colonel Dorland.

"Watch where you're going," he said.

He made an attempt to step to the side and continue down the hallway, toward the infirmary. Wahlman pulled out the pistol and pointed it at his face.

"I already know where I'm going," Wahlman said. "Same place you're going."

Dorland stared into the barrel of the gun.

"Are you insane?" he said. "You see this bird on my collar? You better put that weapon away before I stick it up your—"

"Look at me," Wahlman said.

Dorland snarled. The muscles in his jaw were as tight as banjo strings. He looked up and stared into Wahlman's eyes. It took him a few seconds, but then he knew.

His expression relaxed into one of stunned resignation.

"We can work this out," he said.

"I don't think so," Wahlman said.

"What are you going to do? Shoot me? Here?"

"Maybe."

"What do you want?"

"You're going to lead me out of here," Wahlman said. "Then we're going to talk."

"There's too much security. There's no way I can—"

"You have that bird on your collar. And a VIP designation on your ID. You can go anywhere you want to."

"And where exactly is it that I want to go?"

"To your car."

"What makes you think I have a car?"

Wahlman shrugged. "Helicopters flying in and out of here would attract too much attention," he said. "I'm guessing you took the ferry from Myrtle Beach and then drove in on Highway Thirty, just like I did. I'm guessing Highway Thirty is the only way in and out of here by land vehicle. And I'm guessing it's not even a real highway. It's open to the public, but nobody uses it. Because it doesn't go anywhere. It's a dead end. Future toll road. Currently under construction. Right. The dozers and dump trucks are parked out there for looks. Just in case someone—"

"You're pretty smart," Dorland said.

"I'm going to put this pistol back into my pocket, and then I'm going to follow you to the exit. I'll have my hand on the gun the entire time, so don't do anything stupid."

"What if someone tries to stop us?"

"Nobody's going to try to stop us. You're a colonel. I'm a nurse. It's all good."

"We'll have to take one of the capsules," Dorland said.

"What are you talking about?"

"The pneumatic transport system. It's the only way out of the building. I should make it clear right now that I've never actually operated one of those things. I've read the manuals, but I haven't been signed off on—"

"We'll figure it out," Wahlman said. "Move."

Dorland turned around and headed back in the direction he'd come from. Wahlman followed, staying three or four steps behind.

Twenty feet or so from the corner where Wahlman and Dorland had bumped into each other, there was a set of stainless steel doors. Like elevator doors, but wider. Dorland pushed a button and the doors parted, revealing a clear plastic carriage with two bucket seats in it.

"Have you ever ridden in one of these?" Dorland said.

"I'm here, so I must have," Wahlman said. "I guess I was unconscious at the time."

"Climb in, and I'll secure your harness for you."

Wahlman laughed. "You think I'm stupid?" he said. "You climb in first. You're going to be the passenger, and I'm going to be the operator."

"This is not a pony ride at the state fair. These things can be dangerous if you don't know what you're doing."

"Get in. You can tell me what to do. If you touch any of the controls, I will shoot you."

Dorland climbed into the carriage. Wahlman secured the padded harness on that side, instructed him to keep his hands in his pockets.

"Be careful with that gun," Dorland said. "Once we get going, there's going to be an enormous difference in pressure between the inside of the capsule and the outside of the capsule. If you accidentally discharge the weapon—"

"I'm not going to accidentally do anything," Wahlman said. "If I pull the trigger, it's going to be deliberate."

He climbed into the operator's seat and closed the hatch.

"My car's parked in the lot at the rear of the facility," Dorland said. "See the dial that says exterior rear module?"

"Yes."

"Set the dial to seven. Then you'll need to scan my ID and punch today's code into the keypad."

"What if I set the dial to eight? Or nine? Or ten?"

"The higher the number, the faster we'll get there. Seven is standard. The higher numbers are generally only used for extreme emergencies. Believe me, seven is fast enough."

An alarm sounded in the distance. An angry pulsating buzz.

Someone must have alerted the security office. Wahlman figured the hallway outside the carriage would be flooded with soldiers in a matter of seconds. He set the dial to twenty. The max. He reached over and pulled Dorland's ID card out of the plastic sleeve.

"What's the code?" Wahlman said.

Dorland told him the numbers.

Wahlman punched in the code and pressed *ENTER* and off they went, whistling through the darkness. The gravitational pull pinned Wahlman to his seat. He couldn't move. He couldn't have fired the weapon he was holding, even if he'd wanted to. He could barely breathe. It was as if he'd suddenly gained a thousand pounds.

Then it was over. The carriage slowed down for a very brief period, and then it came to an abrupt stop. Wahlman figured the ride had lasted about ten seconds from start to finish. He released his harness and opened the hatch and climbed out.

He stepped over to the passenger side and reached down to help Dorland.

"I thought I was going to pass out," Dorland said.

"Let's go."

"Give me a minute. I don't think I can—"

Wahlman yanked Dorland out of the seat, forced him to stay in front as they exited the wooden shack and stepped out onto a concrete apron.

"Where's your car?" Wahlman said.

"Over there. The blue one."

"Give me the keys."

Dorland reached into his pocket and pulled out a set of keys. He handed them to Wahlman.

"They probably have the exit blocked by now," Dorland said. "They're not going to let you leave the facility alive. You know that, right?"

Wahlman pressed the barrel of the pistol against the back of Dorland's neck and pulled the hammer back. If he wasn't going to be able to leave the facility alive, then Dorland wasn't going to be able to either.

"Walk," Wahlman said.

Dorland stepped down onto the asphalt and started walking toward his car. Wahlman kept the barrel of the pistol pressed against the back of his neck, hyper-focused on moving forward one step at a time. He didn't look to see, but he figured that there were guards up on the roof by now, and he doubted that their rifles were loaded with micro-darts. He figured that their rifles were loaded with high-velocity full-metal-jacket rounds, the kind that would bore a hole the size of a quarter all the way through you faster than you could blink. He figured the back of his skull was in the crosshairs, but he figured he had some leverage. This was a hostage situation now. Nobody was going to take a shot from the roof. Not when it meant risking a senior officer's life. Dorland was a colonel in the United States Army. He was an asset. Heads would roll if anything happened to him. Nobody was going to take a shot. Wahlman was counting on it.

And nobody did.

Wahlman used the transmitter on the key ring to unlock

the car doors and start the engine. He opened the driver side door and forced Dorland to climb over the center console to the front passenger seat, and then he slid into the driver seat and jerked the shifter into gear and pulled out of the parking space. He steered around to the outer edge of the lot, out to the front of the building, out to the front guard shack, which he now realized housed another portal for the pneumatic transport system. There were eight soldiers dressed in full combat gear blocking the traffic lanes on both sides of the shack, four on the entrance side and four on the exit side, all of them facing the little blue electric car Wahlman was driving, all of them aiming their rifles directly at the driver side of the windshield.

Wahlman stepped on the accelerator. He continued forward, toward the right side of the shack. He was relatively certain that the guys standing there wouldn't take any shots, for the same reasons he'd been relatively certain that the supposed rooftop guys wouldn't take any.

But this time he was wrong.

The guards opened up like a firing squad.

18

It was like driving through a sudden hailstorm. Alarming, noisy, damaging to the car's paint and glass.

But ultimately not life-threatening.

"Your car's bulletproof?" Wahlman said.

"Of course," Dorland said, almost cheerfully. "Standard issue for senior officers in the intelligence community. Windows, tires, everything. They would need a tank to stop this vehicle."

Dozens of rounds pinged off the windshield as Wahlman sped forward. The guards on the exit side of the shack jumped out of the way a split second before they became human bowling pins. Wahlman barreled toward the rat-hole-shaped opening at the edge of the woods, navigated the narrow tunnel of foliage, and fishtailed out onto the highway. He headed west, toward town. He'd noticed a couple of good hiding places last night while he was driving around lost. He kept his right hand on the wheel, and he kept his left hand wrapped around the grips of the semi-automatic pistol he'd taken from Major Combs. Finger on the trigger, barrel aimed at Colonel Dorland's core.

"Is there any way to make this thing go faster?" Wahlman said, glancing down at the speedometer, which seemed to be maxing out at eighty miles per hour.

"This thing, as you so eloquently referred to it, is equipped with all sorts of surprises," Dorland said. "One of them is an onboard voice-activated computer that will pretty much do whatever I tell it to do."

"Tell me how to activate it."

"I'm afraid I can't do that."

"Tell me, or I'm going to shoot your ass right now."

"You don't understand. I mean that I literally cannot tell you how to activate the computer. It's programmed to respond to my voice and my voice only."

"Tell it to make the car go faster."

"Eighty is fast enough."

Wahlman raised the pistol and pointed it at Dorland's head.

"Tell it to make the car go faster."

Dorland's jaw muscles tightened again. Wahlman wasn't sure if he was going to comply, or if he was bracing himself to take a bullet in the brain. He was silent for thirty seconds or so, and then he took a deep breath and spoke to the computer.

"Gertrude, please change the maximum cruising speed from eighty miles per hour to one hundred and fifty miles per hour," he said.

"*Changing the maximum cruising speed now*," a pleasant female voice said.

The increased acceleration was immediate and impressive. Speedometer pegged, tachometer jittering nervously along the border where caution met redline.

"What else can your computer do?" Wahlman said. "Is it possible to—"

"Gertrude, please lock all of the doors and windows."

"Locking all doors and windows now."

"Gertrude, please disable the braking system while maintaining the current cruising speed."

"Cruise control set at one hundred and fifty miles per hour. Braking system disabled."

"What are you doing?" Wahlman said.

"Gertrude, please cause this vehicle to self-destruct in exactly five minutes, and remind me how much time is left every minute."

"Self-destruct timer set for five minutes."

Dorland stretched his legs and crossed his ankles and relaxed against the back of his seat.

"Okay, Mr. Wahlman," he said. "If there's something you want to talk to me about, now would be the time."

19

Wahlman shifted his right foot from the accelerator to the brake. Nothing happened. The car continued moving forward at exactly one hundred and fifty miles per hour.

"You have four minutes left on the timer."

Wahlman kept the pistol trained on the left side of Colonel Dorland's head.

"You need to cancel that shit," Wahlman said. "You need to cancel it right now, or I'm going to blow your brains all over the interior of this car."

"Go ahead and shoot me," Dorland said, maintaining his relaxed posture. "Go ahead and throw away your only chance of making it out of this alive."

Dorland was right. He was holding all the cards now.

Wahlman lowered the weapon.

"What's your real name?" he said.

"I don't see how that's relevant, now that you've found me."

"It's going to be relevant when I take the story to the media."

"You have less than four minutes to live. You're not taking the story anywhere."

"If I die, you die," Wahlman said.

"That seems to be the case. At any rate, I'm not telling you my real name. As a member of the intelligence community, it's imperative that I maintain a certain degree of—"

"*You have three minutes left on the timer.*"

Wahlman decided to move on to the next question.

"You've been trying to have me killed for months," he said. "Why?"

"Because I was ordered to have you killed," Colonel Dorland said.

"Okay. But there must have been a reason. You targeted me, and you targeted a man named Darrell Renfro."

"How much do you already know about that?"

"I know you got Renfro. I saw the tractor-trailer he was driving go off a bridge and crash into a canal a few miles east of New Orleans. I tried to save him, but I couldn't. I know that Renfro and I were products of a human cloning experiment, exact genetic duplicates of a former Army officer named Jack Reacher."

"Did you know that you and Mr. Renfro were the first human clones ever produced?"

"No."

"And did you know that no others have been produced since then?"

"No. Get to the point. Why did the Army decide to—"

"That is the point," Colonel Dorland said. "A certain four-star general decided that history needed to be altered a little bit. He made this decision for the reason that a lot of decisions are made, because of money. Our current project is not being funded by the United States government. It's being funded by a group of ordinary citizens—ordinary except for the fact that they're all billionaires. This group has been assured that the human clone soon to be produced in our laboratory is going to be the first in history."

"Why is that so important?" Wahlman said.

"Think about it. Do you remember the name of the second man who walked on the moon?"

Wahlman shrugged. "I guess that's a good point," he said. "But I didn't even know I was a clone when this first started. You could have said whatever you wanted to say about your new project. Nobody would have ever known the difference. There was no reason to kill anyone."

"We couldn't take a chance on you or Mr. Renfro ever finding out about the facts behind your true heritage, couldn't take a chance that those facts might eventually become publicized. It would have exposed us as frauds, and it would have cost us billions of dollars."

"You have two minutes left on the timer."

"I picked up a hitchhiker named Rusty," Wahlman said. "He was coming here for some kind of procedure. What was that all about?"

Dorland was silent for a couple of beats.

"So that's how you found out about the facility," he said. "What did this Rusty fellow tell you?"

"Nothing. He just needed a ride."

"He was supposed to report this morning, no later than

zero seven hundred. What happened to him?"

"Answer my question first," Wahlman said. "Then I'll answer yours."

"Rusty is going to provide the donor cells for our first clone," Dorland said.

"Why him?"

"Because he volunteered. And because his condition is terminal. If something goes wrong during the procedure—"

"Why would anything go wrong?" Wahlman said. "It's a simple blood draw. That was how they harvested the cells from Jack Reacher, right?"

Dorland nodded. "I suppose I should explain that what we're doing now is much different than what they were doing when you and Renfro were born. There was a codename for that project, but it was long and alphanumeric and everyone eventually just started referring to it as The Reacher Experiment. The goal back then was to manufacture super-soldiers. Entire battalions of them. Huge, strong, intelligent. Like Jack Reacher. Like you. It was ambitious, and revolutionary. But it was illegal, and it was costing a fortune, and the administration at the time decided to ditch it in favor of a new line of fighter jets."

"All this stuff is written down somewhere?"

"It was. The files have been destroyed. You and Renfro were the only loose ends. Now it's just you."

"Human cloning is still illegal," Wahlman said.

"Not for long. There's a bill right now in the—"

"I've heard about the bill. It's not going anywhere. The sponsors don't have the votes."

Dorland laughed. "Don't believe everything you read in the newspapers," he said. "The bill will pass, and it will be signed into law. Guaranteed."

"You said that the experiments you're doing now are different from the ones they were doing back when Renfro and I were born. How so?"

"Our project has nothing to do with national defense. It's more of a business venture than anything else. A couple of years ago, one of the principal scientists approached the four-star general I mentioned earlier, and soon after that the four-star general approached me. It's going to make us very wealthy men, and it's going to assure our places in history."

"You have one minute left on the timer."

"I don't know about the general, but in sixty seconds your place in history is going to be a greasy spot on the highway," Wahlman said. "Cancel the timer."

"Give me the gun, and I will."

"I'm not giving you the gun."

"Then I'm not cancelling the timer."

"You're willing to die for this shit?"

"I am."

"You're bluffing."

Dorland laughed. "Do you really think so?" he said.

"Yes," Wahlman said.

"Gertrude, please make the self-destruct timer irreversible, starting now."

"Your last command requires a positive confirmation. You want the self-destruct timer to be irreversible, starting now. Is this correct?"

"Yes," Dorland said. "And please start an audible countdown immediately after executing the next verbal command."

"Audible countdown ready to start following the next verbal command."

Dorland sat up straight, checked his seatbelt.

"You were right," he said. "I was bluffing."

"What are you talking about?"

"Gertrude, please eject the passenger seat now."

The roof receded and Dorland shot out of the top of the car like a rocket. Wahlman glanced into the rearview mirror, saw a parachute open, saw the lines become tangled, saw Dorland dropping like a rock into the forest. It was doubtful that he made it to the ground. He was probably up in the trees somewhere, skewered on some splintered branches, bleeding out slowly and painfully. Wahlman cringed at the thought of it. He couldn't think of a worse way to die.

The roof closed as quickly as it had opened. It mated into the slot at the top of the windshield with a definitive click.

"Twenty-five...twenty-four...twenty-three..."

"This is insane," Wahlman said. "It can't end like this. It just can't."

"Eighteen...seventeen...sixteen..."

"Shut up, Gertrude."

There was a brief pause.

"Discontinuing audible countdown," the computer said.

"Gertrude?"

"Awaiting next verbal command."

Dorland must have been lying about the computer being

programmed to recognize his voice and his voice only. Wahlman felt like an idiot now for taking him at his word.

"Gertrude, discontinue the self-destruct timer."

"*Negative. The command to self-destruct was made irreversible.*"

Shit.

"How much time is left?" Wahlman said.

"*You have eight seconds left on the timer.*"

Shit.

Wahlman considered his options. He had command of the vehicle now. He could use the brakes to come to a complete stop, and he could unlock the doors, and he could unbuckle his seatbelt and climb out and take off running.

But there just wasn't time.

So he did the only thing he could do.

He gave the command, even though he'd seen what had happened to Colonel Dorland.

"Gertrude, eject the driver seat," he said.

And she did.

20

Phoning from a second story hotel room on the outskirts of Myrtle Beach, Wahlman had spoken to ten different investigative reporters at ten different major metropolitan newspapers. Every one of them had told him the same thing. You can't go after a story like that without some kind of proof. Photographs. Documents. Video recordings. Voice recordings. Witnesses willing to come forward and corroborate.

Wahlman had nothing.

He knew for a fact that the Army was planning to conduct secret human cloning experiments out on that island, and he knew that there was more to it than that, but he didn't know any of the details. *It's going to make us very wealthy men, and it's going to assure our places in history.* Dorland had seemed ready to spill it all, but then time had run out.

Wahlman couldn't prove that he'd been captured and held against his will, and there was no physical evidence that any harm had been done to him. He'd watched the fancy little spy car explode from fifty feet in the air, and then he'd floated safely to the grassy area that ran parallel to the shoulder along Highway 30. He'd hiked through the woods and had waited until dark and had paid a rather inebriated fishing boat captain to take him back across the bay. He was fortunate that he'd made it off the island alive, but now all he could think about was going back. He needed more details about what the Army was doing out there, and he needed documentation. Then maybe the media would listen. Maybe they would believe that someone was trying to kill him.

Wahlman knew what he needed to do, but he was getting low on cash and he didn't have a car anymore and the security at the research facility was going to be even more insane now than it had been to start with. So maybe it would be best to just disappear for a while. Maybe hang out in Norfolk for a month or so. Find some sort of work, save some money, take some time to think about how to proceed. Take some time to regroup, keeping in mind that none of this was over yet, that even if Dorland was out of the picture now, someone would be assigned to take his place.

21

General Foss steered into the gravel driveway that ran alongside the cabin, veered off onto the pine needles and parked beside the boxy little hatchback that Colonel Dorland had been issued for his drive back to Tennessee, a no-frills temporary replacement for the ultra-high-tech multimillion-dollar vehicle he had destroyed. Foss climbed out of his SUV, walked around to the back of the cabin and joined Dorland on the deck. Dorland was sitting in a folding chair, staring out at the valley below. There was an orthopedic brace strapped to his left leg and a pair of aluminum crutches leaning against the railing.

"There's a fresh pot of coffee in the kitchen," Dorland said.

"I can't stay. I just wanted to stop by and talk to you for a few minutes. In person. I figured I owed you that."

"Sir?"

"There's a helicopter waiting for me in Nashville. I have some business to take care of in Washington."

"There's a meat and cheese tray in the refrigerator. Case of beer. I thought—"

"I'm relieving you of your command," Foss said. "You are to vacate the premises immediately, and you are to report to the Senior Officer Processing Station in Memphis no later than midnight tonight."

"You're sending me to SOPS?"

"You're off my team. I need people I can trust. You're no longer one of those people."

"General, please. Things just got out of hand for a while. There's no reason we can't—"

"I have nothing else to say to you."

Dorland took a deep breath.

"I'll need some time to pack my things," he said.

"Your uniforms and other personal items will be boxed and shipped to Memphis first thing in the morning. The only thing you need to do right now is to get in your car and drive."

"What about our business venture? I have a lot of time and money invested in—"

"You'll be reimbursed. We're going to need for you to sign some non-disclosure agreements. I'm sending a man to SOPS to talk to you about all that. He should be there tomorrow."

Dorland reached up and grabbed the deck railing, pulled himself to a standing position.

"All I can say is that I'm sorry," he said.

"Get out of my sight," Foss said.

Colonel Dorland grabbed the crutches and positioned them under his arms and crossed the deck. He turned and saluted, and then he walked through the cabin and exited through the front door.

General Foss pulled his cell phone out of his pocket and pressed the *SEND* button on a text message he'd composed earlier. He heard Dorland start the boxy little hatchback, and he heard the sound of rubber on gravel as he backed out of the driveway. And that was all he heard. He didn't hear Dorland skidding to a stop when he got to the roadblock a mile or so down the mountain, and he didn't hear Dorland shout and scream as he was being dragged out of his vehicle and forced to walk into the woods. He didn't hear any of that, and he certainly didn't hear the gunshot that drove a bullet into Dorland's brain, because the lieutenant he'd sent the message to—a promising young deep encryption expert named Driessman—always used a sound suppressor on these types of occasions.

Thanks so much for reading REDLINE!

For occasional updates and special offers, please visit my website and sign up for my newsletter.

My Nicholas Colt thriller series includes nine full-length novels: COLT, LADY 52, POCKET-47, CROSSCUT, SNUFF TAG 9, KEY DEATH, BLOOD TATTOO, SYCAMORE BLUFF, and THE REACHER FILES: FUGITIVE (Previously Published as ANNEX 1).

THE REACHER FILES: VELOCITY takes the series in a new direction, and sets the stage for THE BLOOD NOTEBOOKS.

And now, for the first time, 4 NICHOLAS COLT NOVELS have been published together in a box set at a special low price.

All of my books are lendable, so feel free to share them with a friend at no additional cost.

All reviews are much appreciated!

Thanks again, and happy reading!

Jude

Made in the USA
Lexington, KY
13 May 2019